MIDNIGHT FAE ACADEMY

THE ADULT COLORING BOOK

LEXI C. FOSS

ILLUSTRATED BY ARNILD C. ALDEPOLLA

Midnight Fae Academy: The Adult Coloring Book

Editing by: Outthink Editing, LLC

Cover Design by: Arnild C. Aldepolla

Coloring Book Page Illustrations by: Arnild C. Aldepolla

Published by: Ninja Newt Publishing, LLC

Print Edition
ISBN: 978-1-68530-080-7

WELCOME TO MIDNIGHT FAE ACADEMY.
HOME OF THE DARK ARTS.
VAMPIRES.
AND CRUELLY HANDSOME FAE.

1
MIDNIGHT FAE
ACADEMY

"Stop," I managed to say,
my demand lost to the raspy quality of my tone.

He chuckled against my neck,
his tongue darting out to tease my racing pulse.

"I wish I could, delicate flower.
But I've been given a task. *You.*"

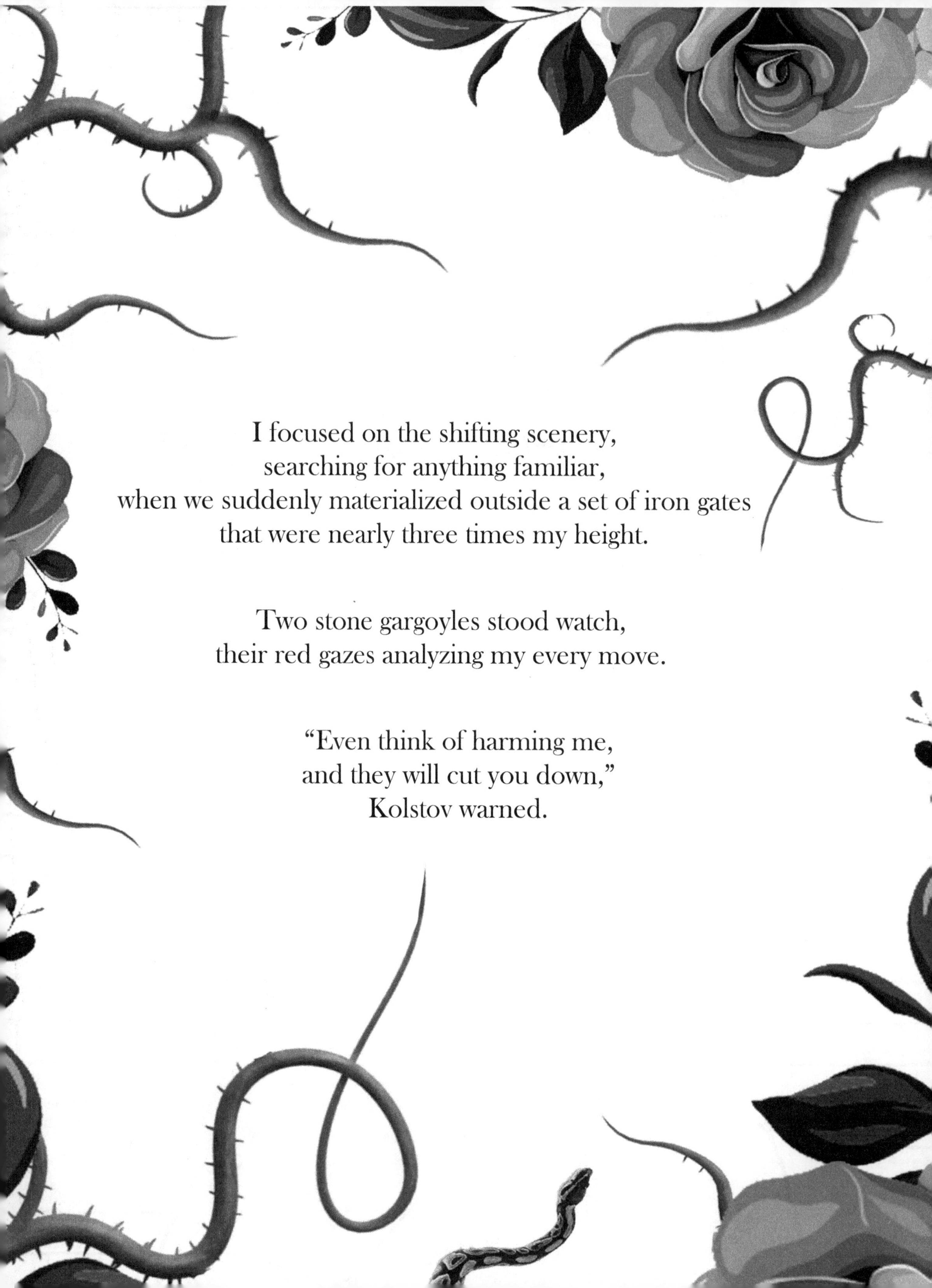

I focused on the shifting scenery,
searching for anything familiar,
when we suddenly materialized outside a set of iron gates
that were nearly three times my height.

Two stone gargoyles stood watch,
their red gazes analyzing my every move.

"Even think of harming me,
and they will cut you down,"
Kolstov warned.

"Aflora!" Kolstov yelled.

My lips curled, power rippling through me in energizing waves.

What was it he said to me earlier? Oh, right.

"I'm ready to dance now, Midnight Prince," I told him,
shoving him away with a pulse of energy that put him on his ass.

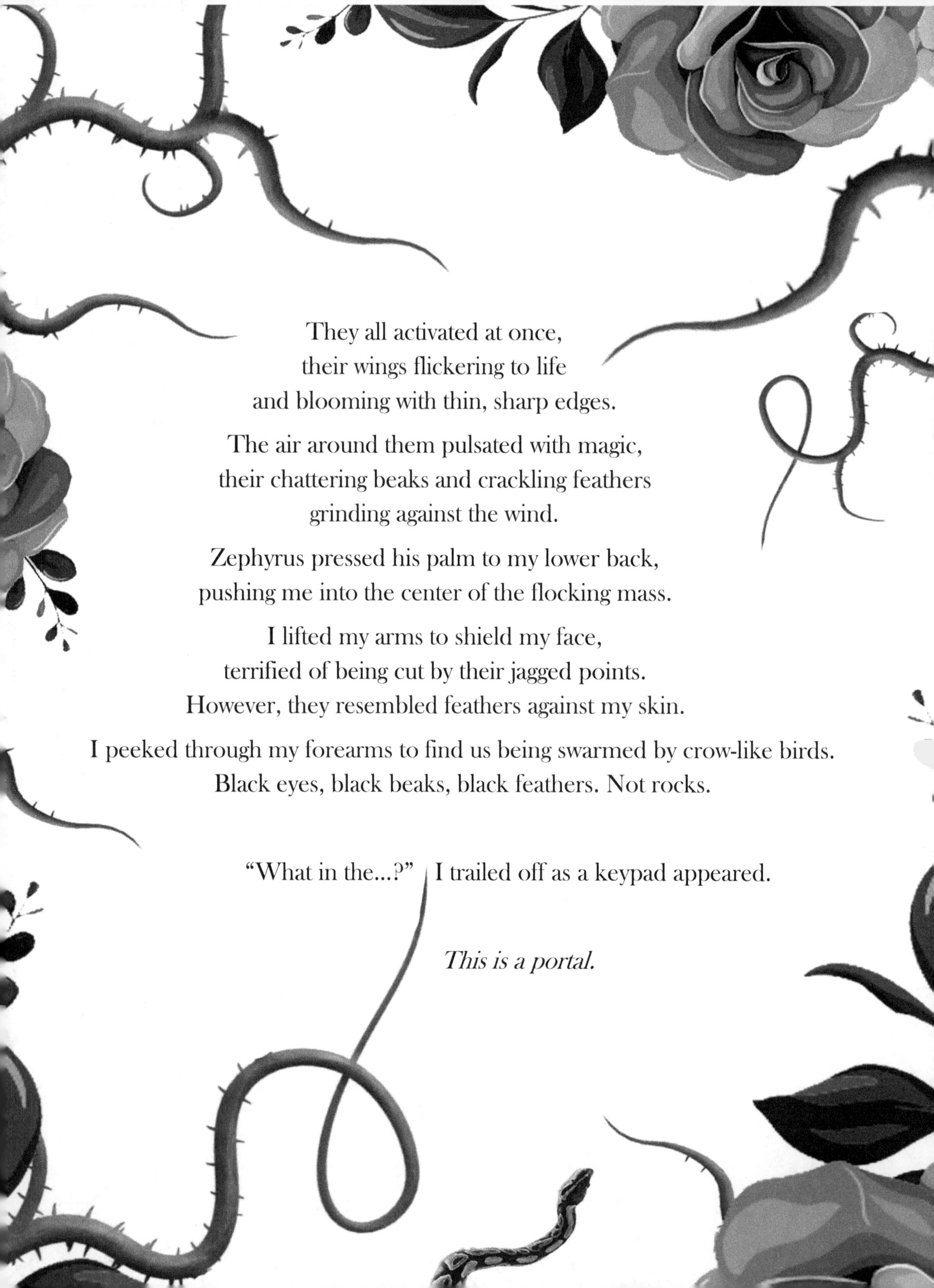

They all activated at once,
their wings flickering to life
and blooming with thin, sharp edges.

The air around them pulsated with magic,
their chattering beaks and crackling feathers
grinding against the wind.

Zephyrus pressed his palm to my lower back,
pushing me into the center of the flocking mass.

I lifted my arms to shield my face,
terrified of being cut by their jagged points.
However, they resembled feathers against my skin.

I peeked through my forearms to find us being swarmed by crow-like birds.
Black eyes, black beaks, black feathers. Not rocks.

"What in the...?" I trailed off as a keypad appeared.

This is a portal.

One hand remained against my hip
while his opposite rose to my hair,
his fingers entangling in my strands
as he tilted my head to better receive his kiss.

Some part of me was screaming at us to stop.

But I couldn't hear her over the roar of need in my thoughts.

Heat unlike anything I ever remembered feeling seared my insides,
pulsing through my veins with one driving thought—*more*.

I took out my wand as well,
unsure of how that would help me,
and waited for her next attack.

Which came in the form of a water figment
shaped like a lion.
I jumped to the side as its jaws yawned wide,
its teeth far too real.
They reminded me of crystal fragments.
Sharp, precise, and turning right for me.

A cerulean wave of power billowed out of me,
destroying her fragment
and sending Ella to the ground.

I jumped backward, the two animals lunging for one another at
the same time and squabbling across the ground.

"Stop!" I demanded,
trying to pull the slithering monster off my falcon.
It had all three sets of mouths latched onto different points,
its tail wrapping around the body to squeeze
as Clove's talons dug into the scaly rope
and tried to use its beak to pierce the slimy beast.

"Make them stop!" I begged him, tears pouring from my eyes.
But he merely watched the show with a disinterested expression,
his green irises as dead as his soul.

She shuddered,
her sweet breath a kiss I could no longer deny.
I captured her mouth on her next inhale, my tongue sliding in
to duel with hers a hairsbreadth of a second later,
and our worlds came crashing down together in unison.

I felt the intrusion deep inside, the rightness of our embrace
locking us together in an intimacy that would never end.

She was beneath me in the next moment, my hips settling
between hers as I pinned her to the bed.

"Help me," I begged,
not sure if I spoke the words out loud
or muttered them in my mind.

"Too hot. Dying."

An agonized cry reached my ears,
the sound excruciating, one I belatedly realized was my own.

Everything glimmered in shades of blue around me,
a rippling effect of my overheated aura.

I ripped at the choker around my neck, needing my earth,
hoping to hide in the source to find my stability once more.

"Now!" Kols demanded. "Before she detonates again!"

Again? I thought, wincing as something sharp pinched my neck.
Shade, I recognized immediately.

I gasped as Kols bit the other side of my neck,
his incisors sliding deep into my vein to suck harshly at my blood.

A cry lodged in my throat, the pain mingling with pleasure
as a third mouth met my breast, the kiss almost gentle.
The slice of teeth followed against my tender skin,
causing my back to bow off the ground.
Zeph.

All three of them pulled in unison, taking my blood

and leaving me   weak

and

defenseless

beneath them.

The door to the bedroom crashed open,
two Midnight Fae charging in with wands at the ready.

Zeph leaned against the wall, his hands in his pockets,
as Kols followed what I now realized were Royal Guardians.

They wore the Nacht family crest on their cloaks,
the green colors denoting them as Warrior Bloods.

Just like Zeph.

"She's disarmed," Zeph informed them, his tone dead and emotionless.
"As requested."

What?

"Excellent. Take her to the Council dungeons,"

Kols said, sounding as regal as ever.

2
MIDNIGHT FAE
ACADEMY

I rubbed a hand over my face
as the iron bars locked behind Aflora,
the gargoyle overhead watching her with severe distaste.
"Don't harm her," I told the stone creature. "She's still a guest
until the Council deems otherwise."

Aflora snorted before settling on a stone bench,
her eyes continuing to avoid mine.

There were things I wanted to say
but couldn't with our surrounding audience.
So I merely said,
"Someone will return should a test of your abilities be required
for the trial."

He'd purposely brought me here and was telling me the lie
he intended to give everyone else.

My fingers unfurled from the fists at my sides,
realization threatening to breach the icy confines of my heart.
He brought me here to play with my earth.

He'd given me the gift of the sun. The grass. Trees with real leaves.
Flowers in full bloom.

"Use your Quandary Blood to set your earth source free, little rose,"
he murmured. "I've always favored floral scents."

A gargoyle crawled up onto our table, his expression bored.
"What'll it be?"

"Three spritemeads, please," Ella said. "And some menus."

"Yeah, yeah," the stone creature grumbled before jumping down
with a loud crunch as his stone feet met the marble floor.

I winced, thinking that sounded rather painful,
but his wings crinkled at his back as he strutted off toward the bar.

Zeph's grip tightened around me, his warmth bleeding into me, wrapping me in a cocoon of safety. *Literally.*

I blinked, realizing his magic poured out of him in a defensive shield, covering not just me but all the students in the field.

I peeked around him to find Kols at the other end, his own power connecting to Zeph's to bolster him in his effort in protecting the entire class from the debris and insanity flying overhead.

"We're going to play a game, Aflora,"
he informed her softly.

"What kind of game?" she asked, her voice holding a sultry quality
to it that made my blood pump a little faster.

"One where you guess who is touching you," he murmured,
trailing my silk tie up her neck. "If you're right, we'll reward you."
The garment met her cheek. "And if you're wrong, we'll teach you."

"Teach me?" she repeated, her tongue sneaking out to lick her bottom lip.
"Teach me what?"

"You'll see," he replied, draping the fabric over her forehead, preparing
to slide it down. "Now close your eyes. We're about to begin."

Who are you?

You know me, he vowed. *You'll see.*

I didn't understand, but an inferno blazed all around me,
making me hot and cold at the same time.
Shivers racked me from head to toe, my lips parting
on another one of those silent screams.

And then we were outside, our hand rising into the sky to script out
a word I already knew was meant to be written.

"Alqisian," I whispered at the same time as the male,
our voices commingling into a beautiful song I couldn't help but hum.

Magician

Our fate.

I couldn't even begin to explain that to her.

All I could do was continue to guide her and allow her to make her own decisions. Like she did tonight when she bit me.

I drew my mouth to hers once more, kissing her thoroughly and thanking her with my tongue for the gift of her bond. She would never know how much it meant to me. Or maybe she'd sense it.

Regardless, it was done.

We belonged to each other.

Who are you? I demanded,
the words in my mind
rather than out loud.

Your destiny, a deep, sensual voice replied. *My darling Aflora,
you truly have grown into a beautiful woman.
Just like your mother.*

Another kiss of power touched my heart, working its way through my blood,
heating all my frozen limbs beneath a ripple of authority and awareness.

I tried to track him, but he lingered in the shadows,
his presence there and gone in the breeze.

We'll play again soon, he promised darkly. *Retribution will be ours.*

I enjoyed how Zeph felt
as he trapped me between his body
and the hard surface behind me.

"Yes," I said softly, my hands wandering up to grasp Zeph's
shoulders. "I like that plan very much."

"Do you?" he asked, his words a breath against my ear. "It won't be
sweet or romantic, but hard and fast. It might hurt."

"Will you bite me?" I asked him.

"If you want me to."

"I do."

"It'll finalize our mating bond," he warned.

"I know."

"Aflora!" Emelyn shouted again, fear etched into her voice.

A rock creature of some kind came toward her,
the fingertips long talons of black flames.

It lashed out at her, catching her wrist.

She cried out in pain, her spells no match for the monster.

I forced myself to my feet, careful of the surrounding terrain,
and searched for my wand.

"What did you do?" I asked, shivering
uncontrollably despite the warm sun overhead.
"What did you do, Shade?"

"What fate required me to do," he replied against my ear,
his lips brushing my temple.
"I warned you that you would hate me. Now you know why."

"Because you're working with *him*?"
But I didn't even really know what that meant.
This male had attacked the Academy, seduced me in my dreams,
tried to trap me in the village, and now stared at me with almost illicit intent.
"Who are you?" I asked him. "Why are you doing this?"

"I'm Zakkai," he replied. "As to why I'm doing this, well..."
He smiled, pushing off the tree to saunter toward me.

3
MIDNIGHT FAE
ACADEMY

A jolt radiated through my blood,
sending me to my knees as Shade retaliated
far faster than he should have been able to react.
Fuck!

I yanked on the source, preparing another attack
as he phased behind me *again*.

He shouldn't have been able to do that.

He should have been knocked out, on his ass, for at least another—

"Fine. We'll do it your way," he said against my ear.

Then his teeth sank into my neck,
causing me to sputter out a surprised curse.

Stars twinkled overhead,
each one tied to an invisible strand
that I sensed more than saw.

I studied them,
searching for a pattern or some reason for the madness.
Zakkai had locked me inside this riddled web,
his power potent and breathtakingly beautiful.

I wanted to roll in his essence and absorb all of it into my senses.

Each star possessed a heat signature that sang to the dark magic inside me.
Zakkai's magic. He was the source of my Quandary skills.
But how? When had we bonded? And why didn't I remember?

"Who the hell taught you how to duel?"

"Zephyrus," she replied,
sending another blast of magic at my torso that resembled red flames.
"And Kols."
She disappeared into a cloud of purple smoke,
only to appear behind me with a ball of fiery violet energy.
"And *Shade*."

She unleashed the WarFire directly at my head.

Right.

She wasn't dueling.

She was trying to kill me.

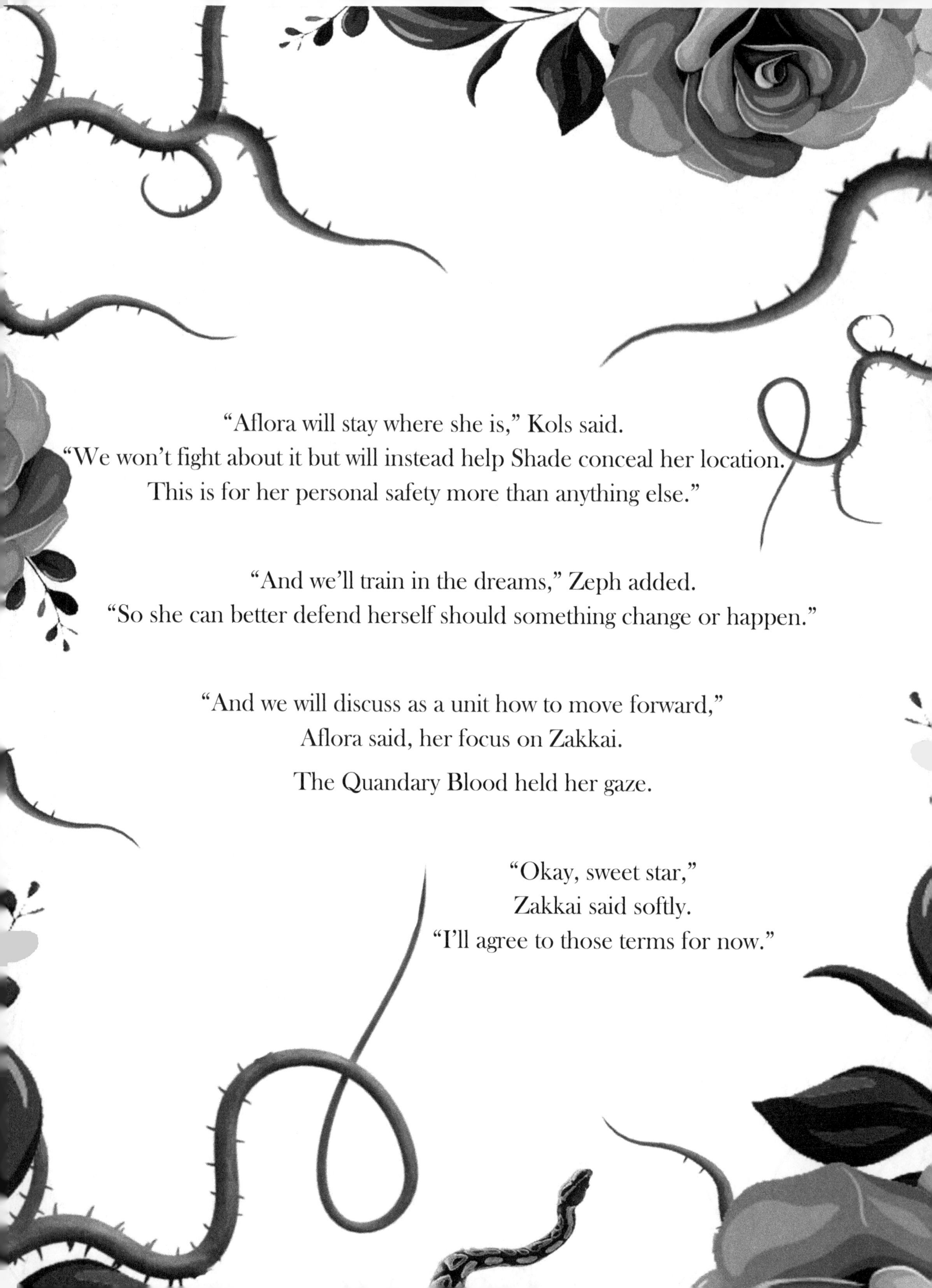

"Aflora will stay where she is," Kols said.
"We won't fight about it but will instead help Shade conceal her location.
This is for her personal safety more than anything else."

"And we'll train in the dreams," Zeph added.
"So she can better defend herself should something change or happen."

"And we will discuss as a unit how to move forward,"
Aflora said, her focus on Zakkai.

The Quandary Blood held her gaze.

"Okay, sweet star,"
Zakkai said softly.
"I'll agree to those terms for now."

"Use me," I told him. "Take it out on me."

"No."

"Do it, Zeph."
I wrapped my hand around the back of his neck
and grabbed his hip with my opposite palm.
"Destroy me."

"*No.*"

"Stubborn dick," I said, crushing my mouth against his.

He threaded his fingers through my hair, yanking hard to pull me away,
but I sank my teeth into his lower lip to hold on.

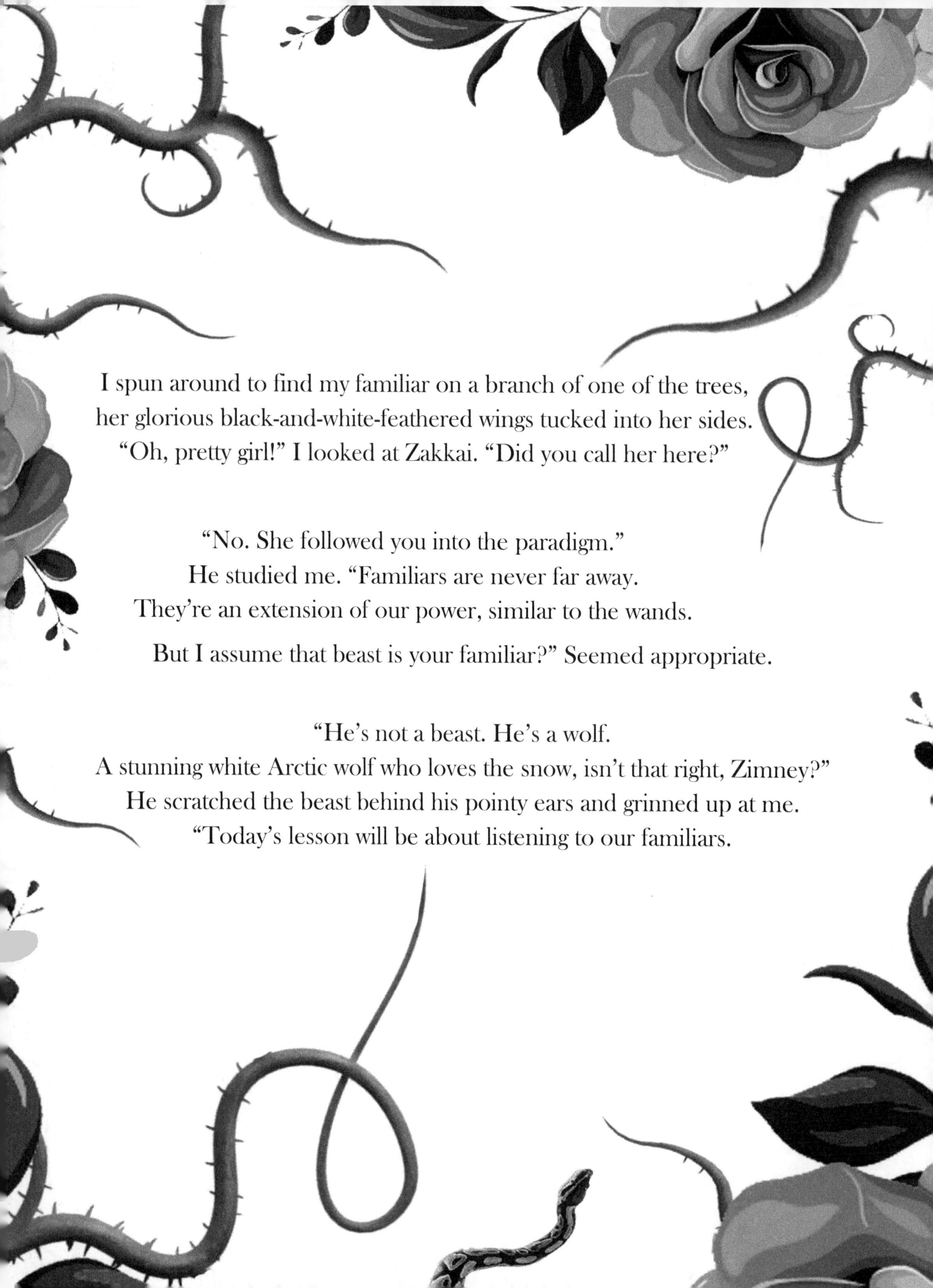

I spun around to find my familiar on a branch of one of the trees,
her glorious black-and-white-feathered wings tucked into her sides.
"Oh, pretty girl!" I looked at Zakkai. "Did you call her here?"

"No. She followed you into the paradigm."
He studied me. "Familiars are never far away.
They're an extension of our power, similar to the wands.

But I assume that beast is your familiar?" Seemed appropriate.

"He's not a beast. He's a wolf.
A stunning white Arctic wolf who loves the snow, isn't that right, Zimney?"
He scratched the beast behind his pointy ears and grinned up at me.
"Today's lesson will be about listening to our familiars.

"So you think there's a way to align all the factions?"
Aflora was saying beside me.

She sat between me and Shade at Zenaida's dining room table.

The Fortune Fae Omega and her two mates were seated across from us.

It was almost like looking into the future to see where we
would be in a thousand years, except Aflora would argue
that we were missing Zephyrus and Kolstov.

Zakkai gently drew the chain around my throat, allowing the pendant to hang along my breastbone, and clasped the chain at my nape. "How does it feel?"

"Like a necklace," I whispered.

"Dad?"

Laki pursed his lip. "The beacon of power has dimmed."

Zakkai grinned. "This will hide your mating bonds as well." He showed me a watch on his wrist. "Just like this is hiding my link to you, in addition to dulling my power."

I frowned down at the beautiful charm. "But I don't feel any different." "Good. That means my spell worked." He stepped to my side, his attention on his father. "Anything else, Dad?"

"It's a risk."

"So was taking me seven years ago," Zakkai murmured. "She needs to see this just like I did."

My knees buckled beneath the impact,
the air whooshing from my lungs.
No! I pushed back,
creating a shield to protect myself against the onslaught,
but it was too late.

Dark energy rippled along my arms,
the source calling upon my spirit to relinquish control.
It hit me from inside, spreading a sharp demand through my veins,
sucking the life from my very soul.

"You're killing him!" Ella screamed.

Tears streamed from my eyes, my vision blurring
as I attempted to yank some of the power back into my veins,
my soul screeching in anguish at having my essence
ripped from me without permission.

Energy rippled out of me,
pouring into the ground
as I released all my fury and pain and anguish.
I was done. *So done*!

I hated them all.

They would *burn*.

Flames shot from my fingertips, scorching the ground.

Shrieks followed.

Power rippled.

And still, I unleashed, furious at those who had harmed me and mine.

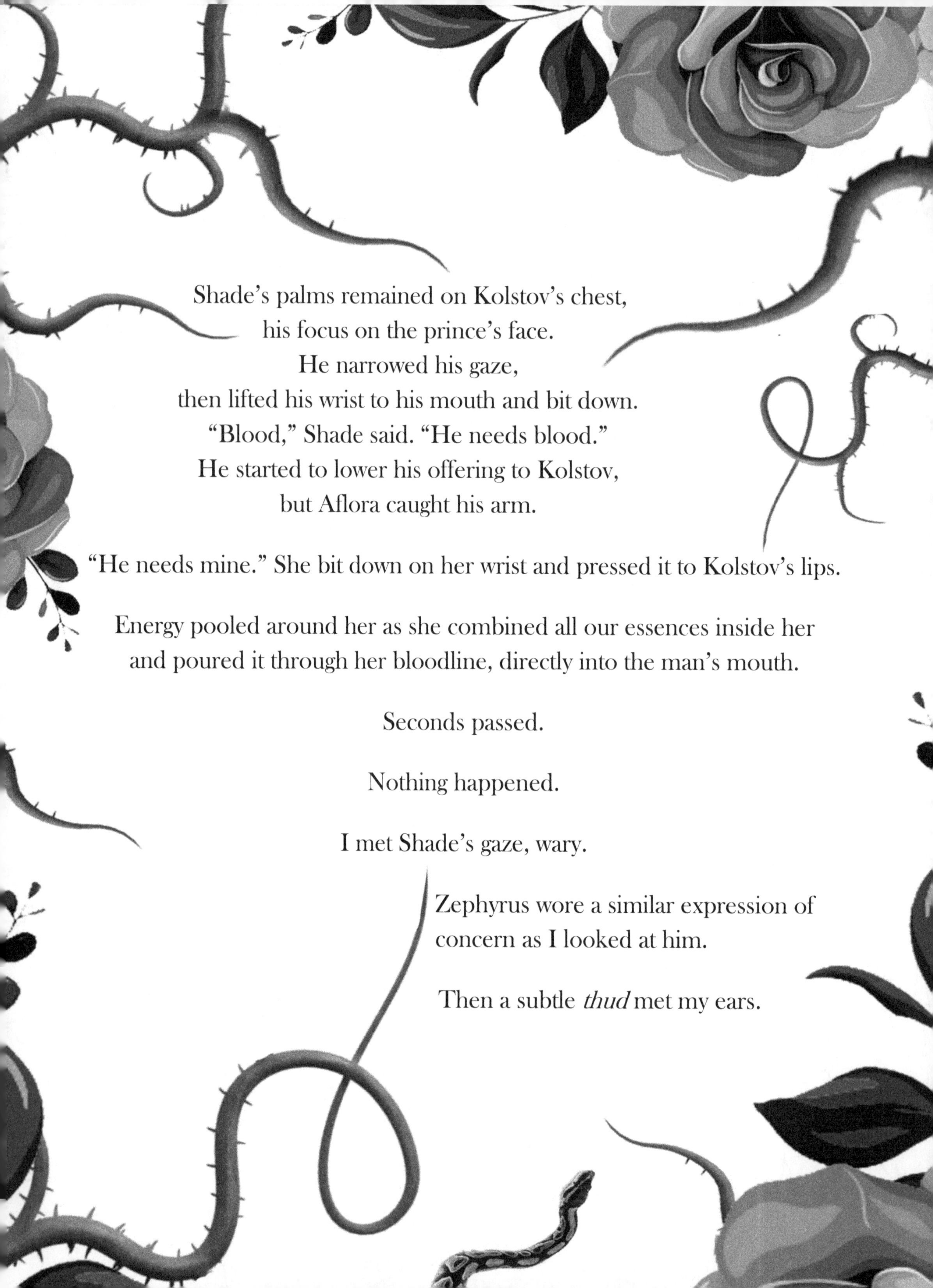

Shade's palms remained on Kolstov's chest,
his focus on the prince's face.
He narrowed his gaze,
then lifted his wrist to his mouth and bit down.
"Blood," Shade said. "He needs blood."
He started to lower his offering to Kolstov,
but Aflora caught his arm.

"He needs mine." She bit down on her wrist and pressed it to Kolstov's lips.

Energy pooled around her as she combined all our essences inside her
and poured it through her bloodline, directly into the man's mouth.

Seconds passed.

Nothing happened.

I met Shade's gaze, wary.

Zephyrus wore a similar expression of
concern as I looked at him.

Then a subtle *thud* met my ears.

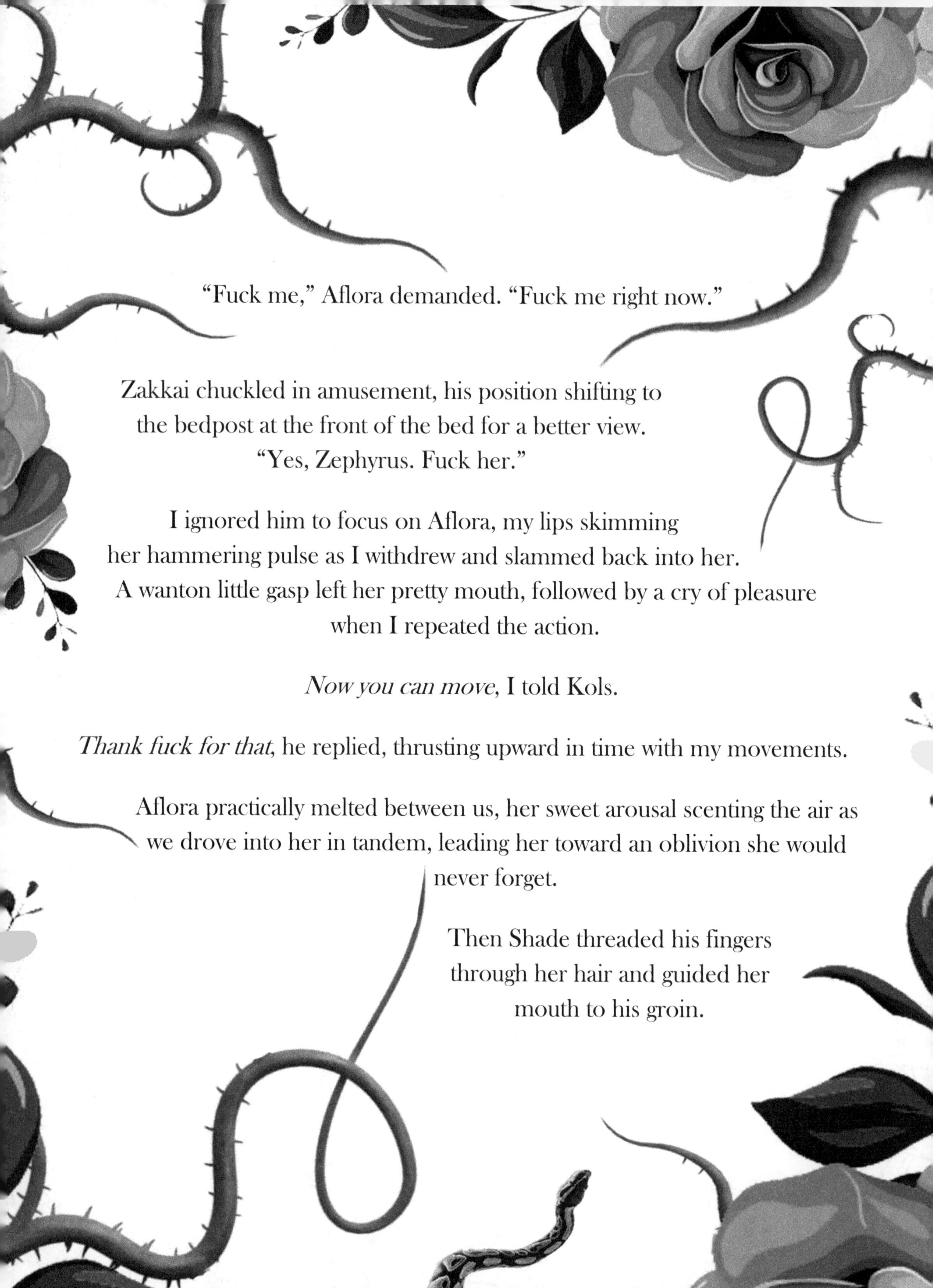

"Fuck me," Aflora demanded. "Fuck me right now."

Zakkai chuckled in amusement, his position shifting to
the bedpost at the front of the bed for a better view.
"Yes, Zephyrus. Fuck her."

I ignored him to focus on Aflora, my lips skimming
her hammering pulse as I withdrew and slammed back into her.
A wanton little gasp left her pretty mouth, followed by a cry of pleasure
when I repeated the action.

Now you can move, I told Kols.

Thank fuck for that, he replied, thrusting upward in time with my movements.

Aflora practically melted between us, her sweet arousal scenting the air as
we drove into her in tandem, leading her toward an oblivion she would
never forget.

Then Shade threaded his fingers
through her hair and guided her
mouth to his groin.

4
MIDNIGHT FAE
ACADEMY

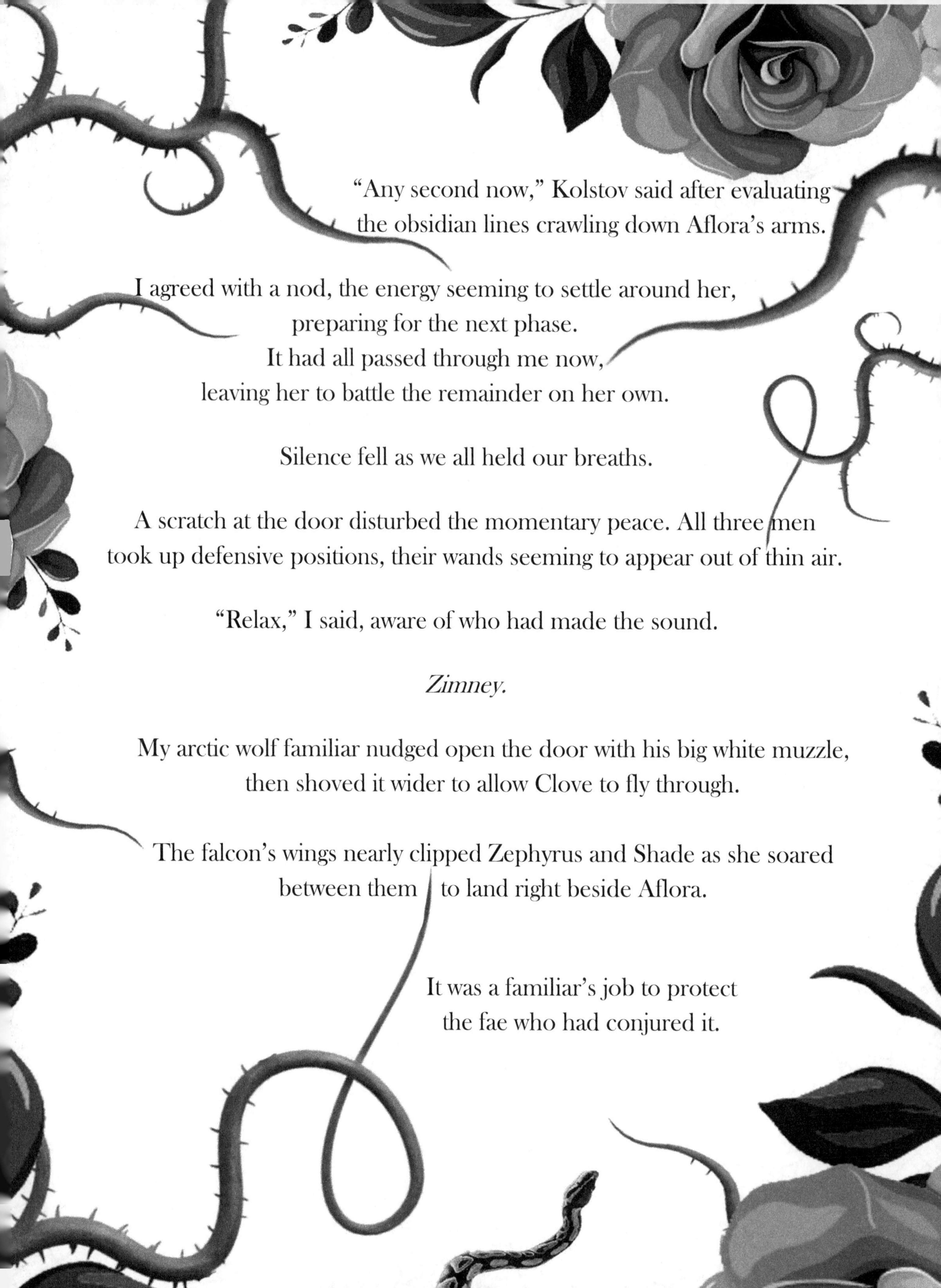

"Any second now," Kolstov said after evaluating
the obsidian lines crawling down Aflora's arms.

I agreed with a nod, the energy seeming to settle around her,
preparing for the next phase.
It had all passed through me now,
leaving her to battle the remainder on her own.

Silence fell as we all held our breaths.

A scratch at the door disturbed the momentary peace. All three men
took up defensive positions, their wands seeming to appear out of thin air.

"Relax," I said, aware of who had made the sound.

Zimney.

My arctic wolf familiar nudged open the door with his big white muzzle,
then shoved it wider to allow Clove to fly through.

The falcon's wings nearly clipped Zephyrus and Shade as she soared
between them to land right beside Aflora.

It was a familiar's job to protect
the fae who had conjured it.

Kols, Aflora said, drawing me back to the present.
She looked up with her pretty blue eyes,
a smile tugging at the edges of her mouth.
I followed her gaze to find Night hovering above us,
his wings spread wide as he soared in a circle around our heads.

I dropped my arm away from her back and grabbed her hand once more.
"Lead the way," I told him, confident in his ability to guide us out.

Night took off through the mess of feathers, creating a path for us to follow,
and we sprinted after him into the sea of darkness.

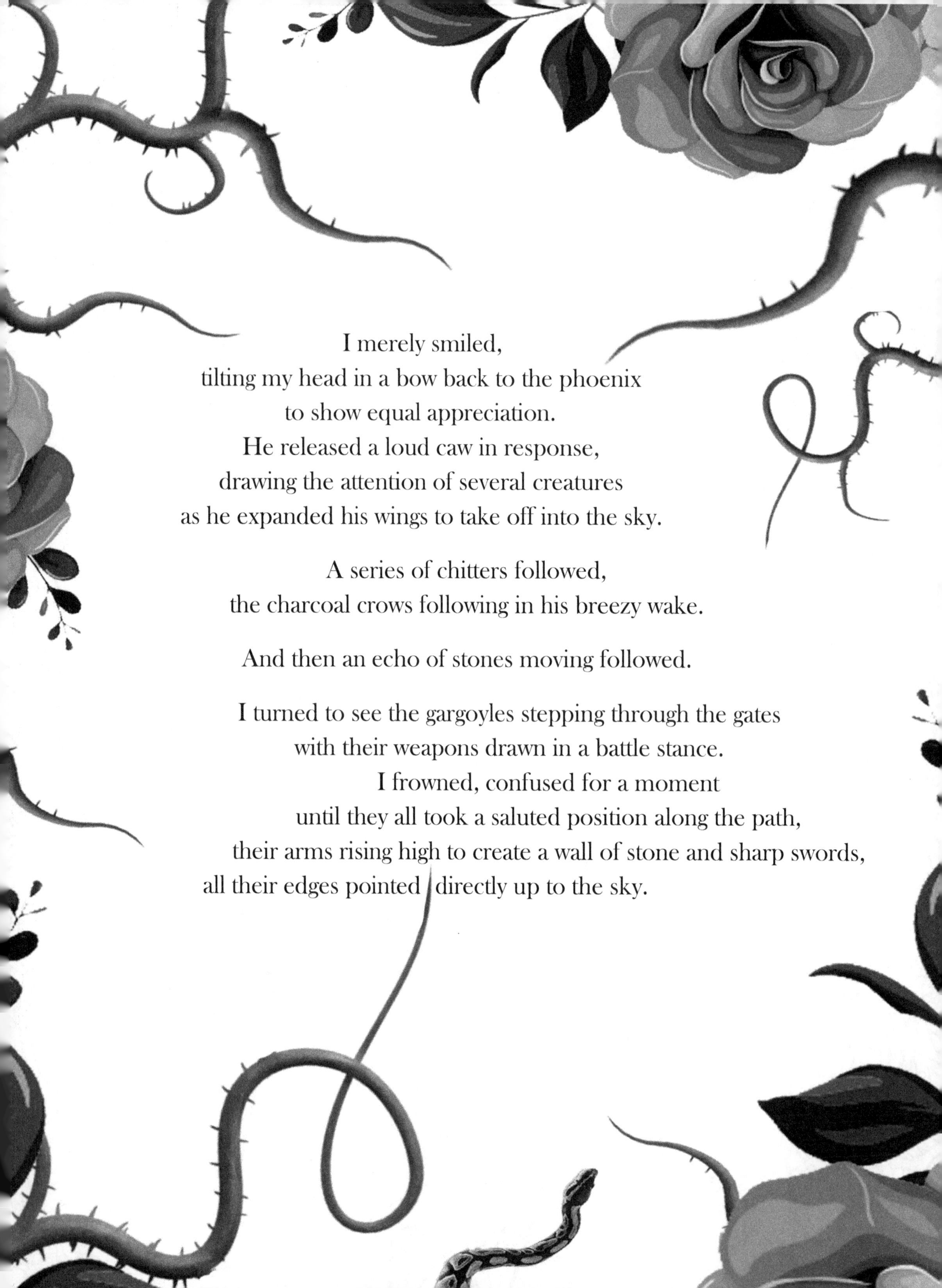

I merely smiled,
tilting my head in a bow back to the phoenix
to show equal appreciation.
He released a loud caw in response,
drawing the attention of several creatures
as he expanded his wings to take off into the sky.

A series of chitters followed,
the charcoal crows following in his breezy wake.

And then an echo of stones moving followed.

I turned to see the gargoyles stepping through the gates
with their weapons drawn in a battle stance.
I frowned, confused for a moment
until they all took a saluted position along the path,
their arms rising high to create a wall of stone and sharp swords,
all their edges pointed directly up to the sky.

Tonight, I needed to complete us.

I prowled forward, crawling over her and caging her beneath me.
"This is about our union," I told her softly,
lowering to press my groin to hers as I balanced myself on my forearms
on either side of her head. "I'm not usually this gentle, Aflora.
But something about the moment requires it."

She reached up to draw her fingers through my hair, the white strands loose
around my face and falling around her like a curtain of false purity.
"I'm not fragile."

"I know," I whispered, pressing my arousal into hers to feel her welcoming heat.
I slipped through her folds, my head nudging her clit before drawing downward
to the heart of her. "But I want to make sure you remember this," I told her,
lining up with her entrance. "And I want to hear you scream my name."

She began to speak,
but her words cut off on a cry
as I drove into her...

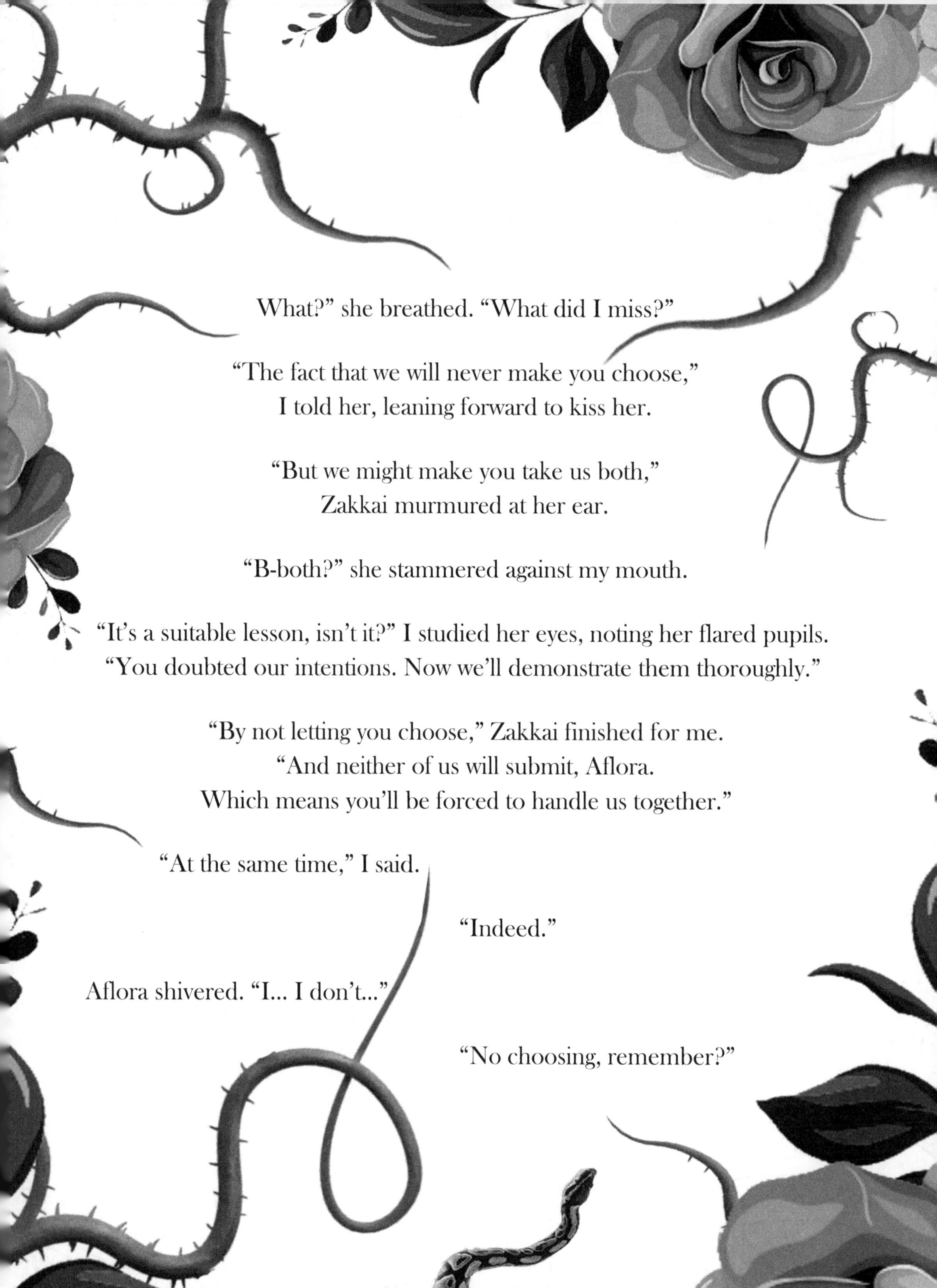

What?" she breathed. "What did I miss?"

"The fact that we will never make you choose,"
I told her, leaning forward to kiss her.

"But we might make you take us both,"
Zakkai murmured at her ear.

"B-both?" she stammered against my mouth.

"It's a suitable lesson, isn't it?" I studied her eyes, noting her flared pupils.
"You doubted our intentions. Now we'll demonstrate them thoroughly."

"By not letting you choose," Zakkai finished for me.
"And neither of us will submit, Aflora.
Which means you'll be forced to handle us together."

"At the same time," I said.

"Indeed."

Aflora shivered. "I... I don't..."

"No choosing, remember?"

Our limbs everywhere. Our mouths dueling.
Our bodies gliding, roaming,
owning each other.

I lost myself to the sensations, drowned in their combined passion,
and gasped when I found them kissing each other.
They were just as lost to the connections as I was,
their tongues mastering one another before sinking their teeth
into each other's necks.

I groaned, the image so erotic and beautiful and intoxicating.

This must have been Constantine's idea of an ideal test.
Sick bastard, I thought,
glaring at his smug face through my shield.

Spells continued to bounce off of it, the edges beginning to fray.

Shadow back, Zakkai urged.

I met Ella's frightened blue eyes on the stage
and noted Tray's lack of a reaction again. *I can't.*

She'd become one of my closest friends.
She'd accepted me before everyone else had. I couldn't leave her.
I'd already failed Emelyn. I wouldn't do the same to Ella.

Because there are good Midnight Fae, I realized.
I was staring into the eyes of one of them and had four more
yelling in my head.

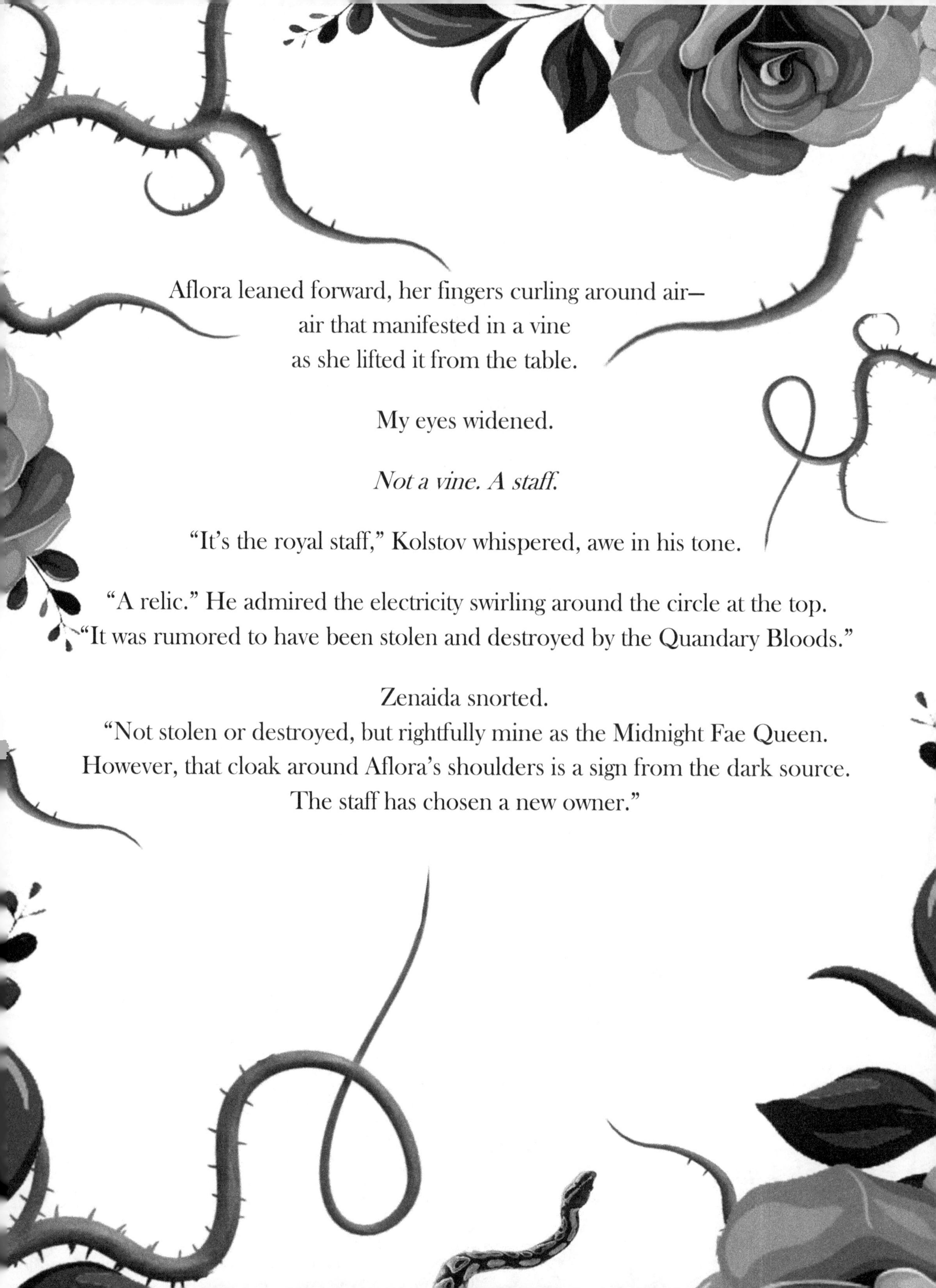

Aflora leaned forward, her fingers curling around air—
air that manifested in a vine
as she lifted it from the table.

My eyes widened.

Not a vine. A staff.

"It's the royal staff," Kolstov whispered, awe in his tone.

"A relic." He admired the electricity swirling around the circle at the top.
"It was rumored to have been stolen and destroyed by the Quandary Bloods."

Zenaida snorted.
"Not stolen or destroyed, but rightfully mine as the Midnight Fae Queen.
However, that cloak around Aflora's shoulders is a sign from the dark source.
The staff has chosen a new owner."

The tree began to grow upward,
the movements measured and controlled by Aflora's power.

"I'm not *naïve*. I'm energy redefined. A queen of two worlds.
An abomination. And a royal who craves creation and life over death.
Midnight Fae have been taught to adore violence for too long.
It's time for an outsider to show them how to live again.
I'm that outsider, the survivor who knows how to fight without bloodshed.
The survivor who knows how to *win* without killing those she's up against."

"The Midnight Fae have forgotten how to love and respect one another,"
she concluded softly, her focus falling to her invention as the roots and branches
began to twine together to form beautiful arrays of color
as their pieces blended and matured as one.
"Together, we can unite the Midnight Fae."

Except, no... those weren't roots.
They're souls, I realized,
recognizing the essence from
Shade's Death Blood magic courses.

The beings twisted in agony,
their hums of magic familiar.

I reached for them on instinct—all four strands—then jolted
as they shot out in all different directions,
their ends securing themselves to the inky walls around me.

What...?

The beings began to stretch, causing me to cry out as they dug their opposite
ends into my palms, their roots deep and solid and joining with my being.
Again. Like they had always been a part of me and it was
the atmosphere around us that had forced me to release them.

What's happening?

"Poor Aflora," the deep voice murmured,
Constantine's tones familiar and recognizable.
"Always choosing her mates over herself."

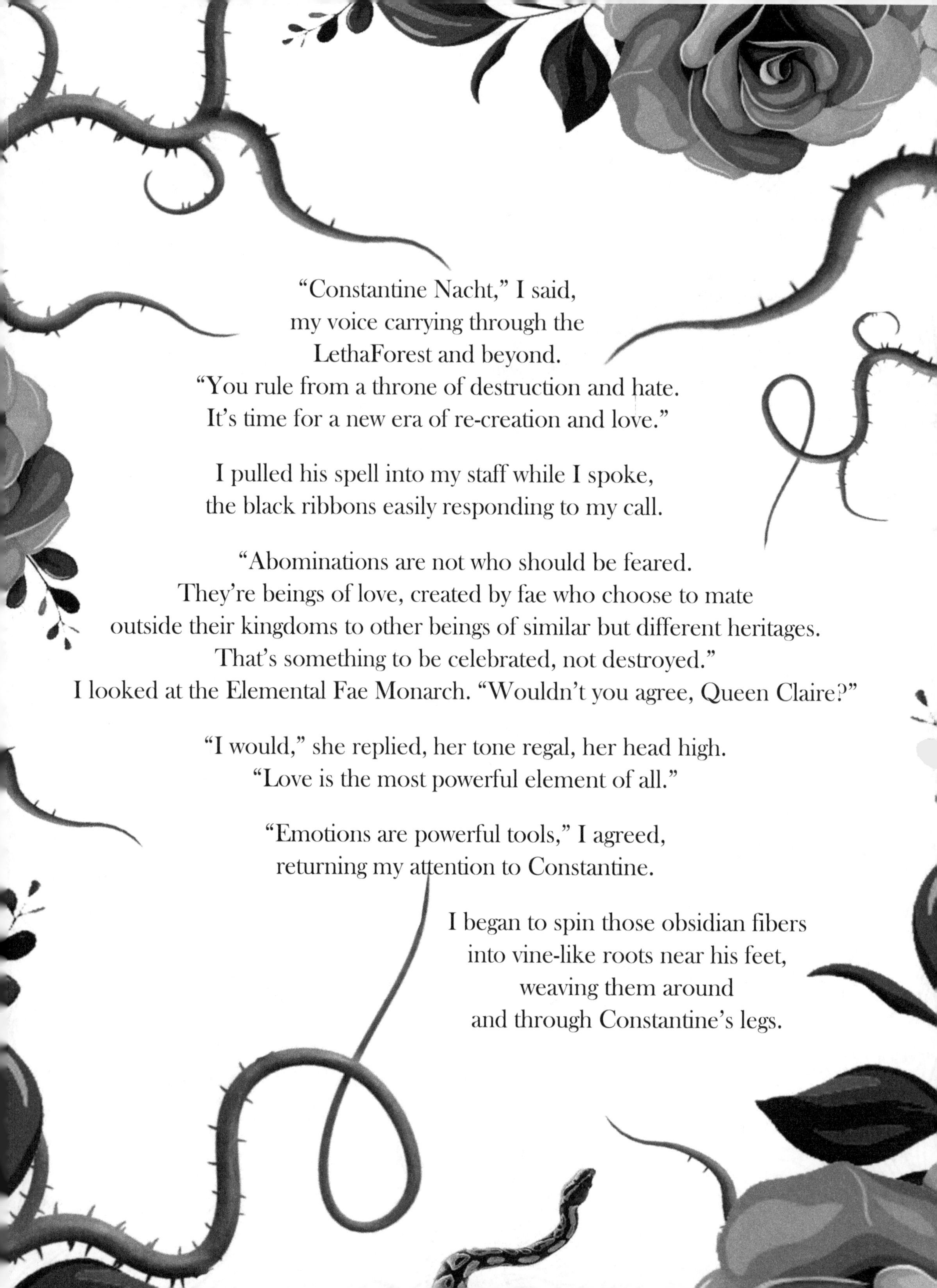

"Constantine Nacht," I said,
my voice carrying through the
LethaForest and beyond.
"You rule from a throne of destruction and hate.
It's time for a new era of re-creation and love."

I pulled his spell into my staff while I spoke,
the black ribbons easily responding to my call.

"Abominations are not who should be feared.
They're beings of love, created by fae who choose to mate
outside their kingdoms to other beings of similar but different heritages.
That's something to be celebrated, not destroyed."
I looked at the Elemental Fae Monarch. "Wouldn't you agree, Queen Claire?"

"I would," she replied, her tone regal, her head high.
"Love is the most powerful element of all."

"Emotions are powerful tools," I agreed,
returning my attention to Constantine.

I began to spin those obsidian fibers
into vine-like roots near his feet,
weaving them around
and through Constantine's legs.

I stood up and waved a spell that disintegrated my clothes.
"Come and get me," I said, taking off for the garden
with a chorus of growls in my wake.

Definitely an amazing life, I thought,
grinning when the first of them caught me
just as I reached the flower bed.
One I wouldn't trade for anything in the world.

Now I knew what it was like to wake from a nightmare
and be fully immersed in a dream.

A dream built to last for an eternity.

With four sexy Midnight Fae mates.

And a future that was entirely our own.

1
MIDNIGHT FAE
ACADEMY
USA TODAY BESTSELLING AUTHOR
LEXI C. FOSS
2
MIDNIGHT FAE
ACADEMY
USA TODAY BESTSELLING AUTHOR
LEXI C. FOSS
3
MIDNIGHT FAE
ACADEMY
USA TODAY BESTSELLING AUTHOR
LEXI C. FOSS
4
MIDNIGHT FAE
ACADEMY
USA TODAY BESTSELLING AUTHOR
LEXI C. FOSS
DON'T MISS